D1368645

One Old
OXFORD OX

Nicola Bayley

A Jonathan Cape Book
ATHENEUM 1977 NEW YORK

Also illustrated by Nicola Bayley

A Book of Nursery Rhymes
The Tyger Voyage
Puss-in-Boots

Library of Congress Cataloging in Publication Data
Bayley, Nicola.
One old Oxford ox.
"A Jonathan Cape book."
SUMMARY: The numbers from one to twelve are presented
by dignified animals and captioned by tongue-twisters.
[1. Counting books] I. Title.
PZ7.B3413On   [E]   77-77866
ISBN 0-689-30608-3

Illustrations copyright © 1977 by Nicola Bayley
Printed in Italy by A. Mondadori Editore, Verona
First American Edition

For Philip

1

One old
Oxford ox
opening oysters

2

Two toads totally tired trying to trot to Tisbury

3

Three thick thumping tigers taking toast for tea

4

Four finicky fishermen fishing for finny fish

5

Five
frippery Frenchmen
foolishly fishing
for frogs

6

Six
sportsmen
shooting snipe

7

Seven
Severn salmon
swallowing shrimps

8

Eight eminent Englishmen eagerly examining Europe

9

Nine nimble
noblemen nibbling
nectarines

10

Ten tinkering tinkers tinkering ten tin tinder boxes

11

Eleven
elephants
elegantly equipped

12

Twelve
typographical
topographers
typically
translating types